Let's Take Care of Our New Frog

Alejandro Algarra / Rosa M. Curto

BARRON'S

We want a frog!

Andrea and Albert are twins and they've decided to ask for a joint present for their birthday. They want a very special pet. It's green and shiny, has very soft damp skin and jumps. Do you know what it is? A frog! The children have seen frogs during the summer in the pond near their house. But especially, they have heard them! "Croak-croak-croak."

Let's choose one

Andrea and Albert's parents have consulted a good pet shop on the Internet to find out which frog is the best for beginners. The best one is the White's tree frog (or "dumpy tree frog"). Today, the four of them went to the shop to choose their pet. The big surprise came when the children found out that they would be able to choose two frogs! When choosing the one they like the best, they simply need to consider that it should look healthy.

Choosing pretty names

The frog that Andrea chose was a very bright green color.
"The best name for a frog of this color is 'Esmeralda,' isn't it Mommy?" said the girl.
The name Albert gave his frog was "Prince." He remembered the story in which the enchanted frog was transformed into a prince when the princess kissed him.

Preparing their house

One day before bringing the pair of frogs home, the children prepared their terrarium:

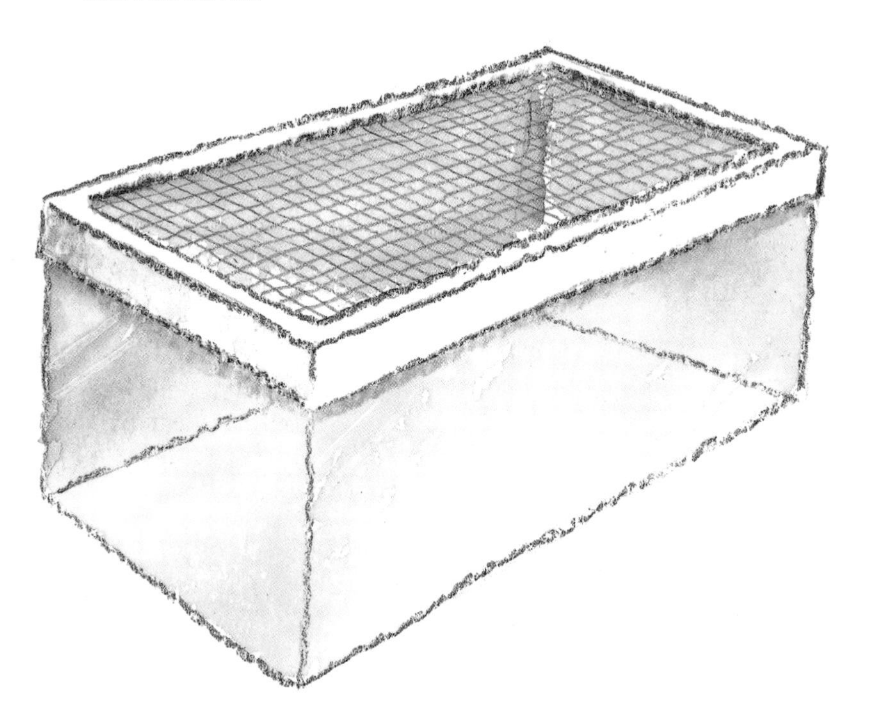

Terrarium: For a pair of frogs, at least 10½ gallons (40 liters) capacity, though bigger is better.
Terrarium cover: If you don't cover their house, your little frogs will escape; the cover is escapeproof and made preferably of nylon mesh.

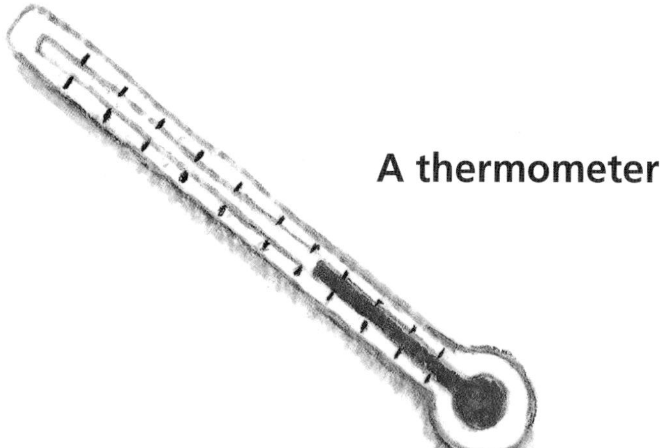

A thermometer

Soil and moss for the ground

Plants: You can either plant them in the soil or place them in small flowerpots; it's better if they have large leaves.

A bath: Put a little water 1–1.5 inches (3–4 cm) in a dish. Change the water when it gets dirty.

Branches and trunks: We can use giant bamboo, trunks and branches; place some of them horizontally so that the frogs can rest in the light.

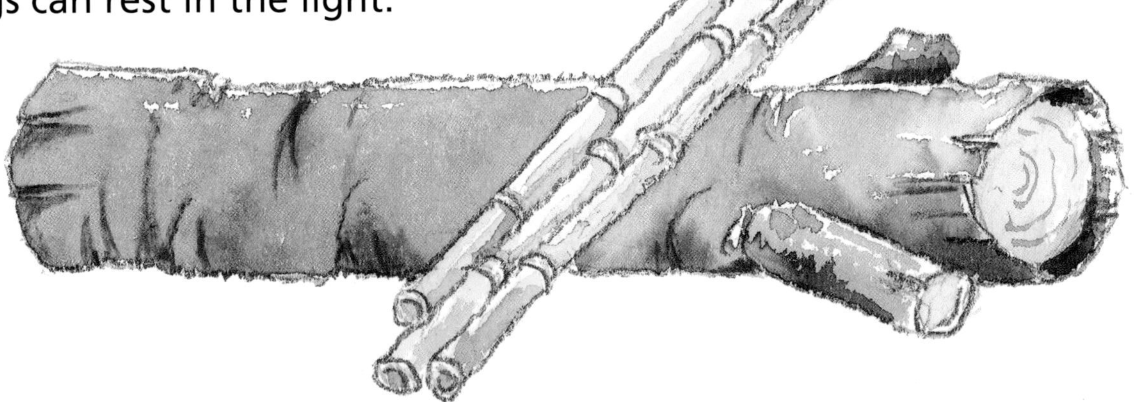

Some very special little frogs

Esmeralda and Prince are two incredible little frogs. They are not like those that Andrea and Albert see in the pond during the summer. More than once, they have found their treefrogs sleeping stuck to the terrarium glass! To be able to do this, they have special feet. The toes end in discs with suction cups, which enable them to walk or cling on almost any surface.

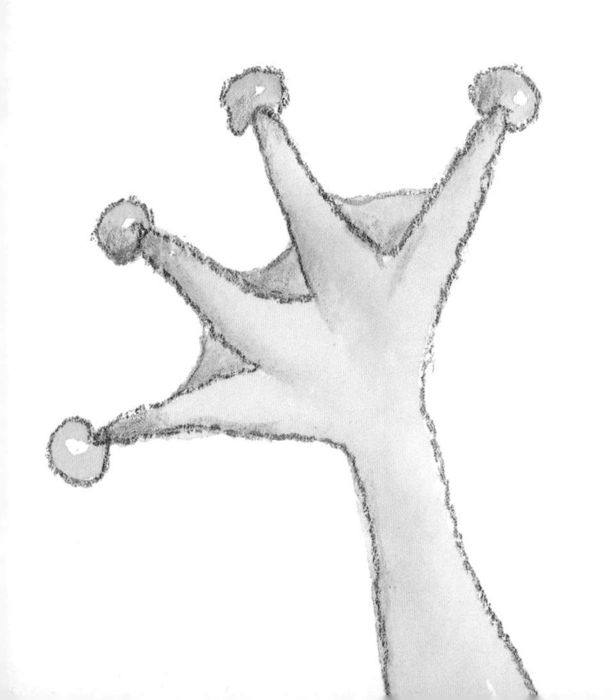

More things for the terrarium

With the help of Mom and Dad, the children have added some very important details to the terrarium. They are things necessary for the frogs to feel comfortable.

A paper cover: The glass should be covered from behind and on the sides (black or decorated paper), so that the little frogs don't feel they are being watched all the time.
Lamp: Can be either a fluorescent or incandescent light bulb type. Care must be taken that the incandescent bulb is far enough from the aquarium top to avoid the frog being accidentally burned—and in a hot room incandescent bulbs may overheat the terrarium. It's important for the terrarium to be illuminated during the day. It also serves to maintain the appropriate temperature.
Humidity: Every day, the terrarium should be sprinkled with water. Not much, just enough to prevent the environment from being too dry, especially during the hot months!

How lovely!

The White's tree frogs are very docile. Andrea and Albert have been able to hold their frogs in their hands from the first day. What a funny feeling, when the frog walks on the palm of your hand! Esmeralda has walked all around Andrea's hand and started to climb up her arm. Be careful! It's best not to let them get near your face! Andrea picks it up very carefully and passes it to Albert.

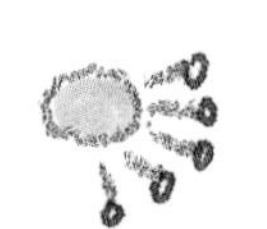

Clean hands

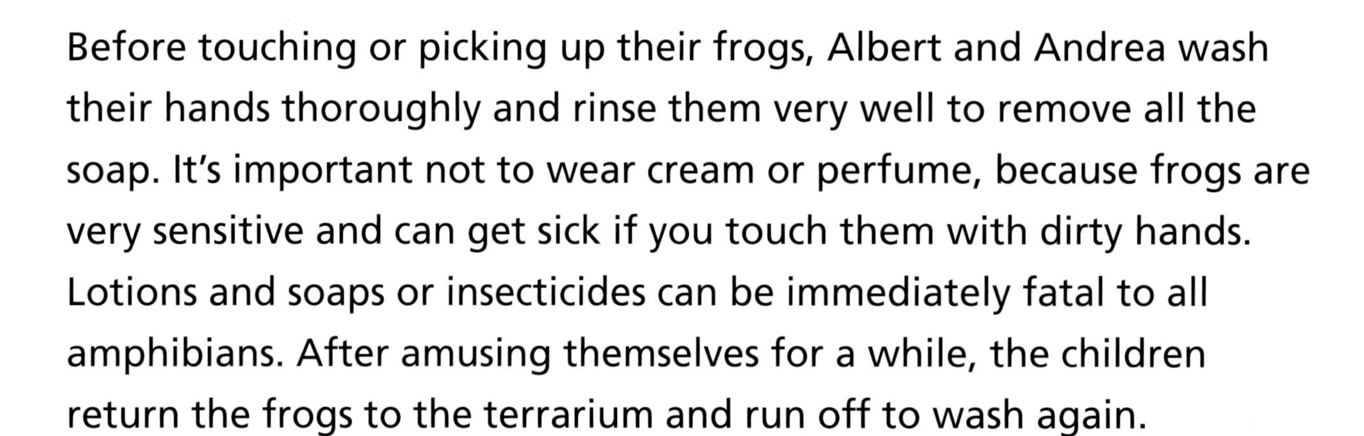

Before touching or picking up their frogs, Albert and Andrea wash their hands thoroughly and rinse them very well to remove all the soap. It’s important not to wear cream or perfume, because frogs are very sensitive and can get sick if you touch them with dirty hands. Lotions and soaps or insecticides can be immediately fatal to all amphibians. After amusing themselves for a while, the children return the frogs to the terrarium and run off to wash again.

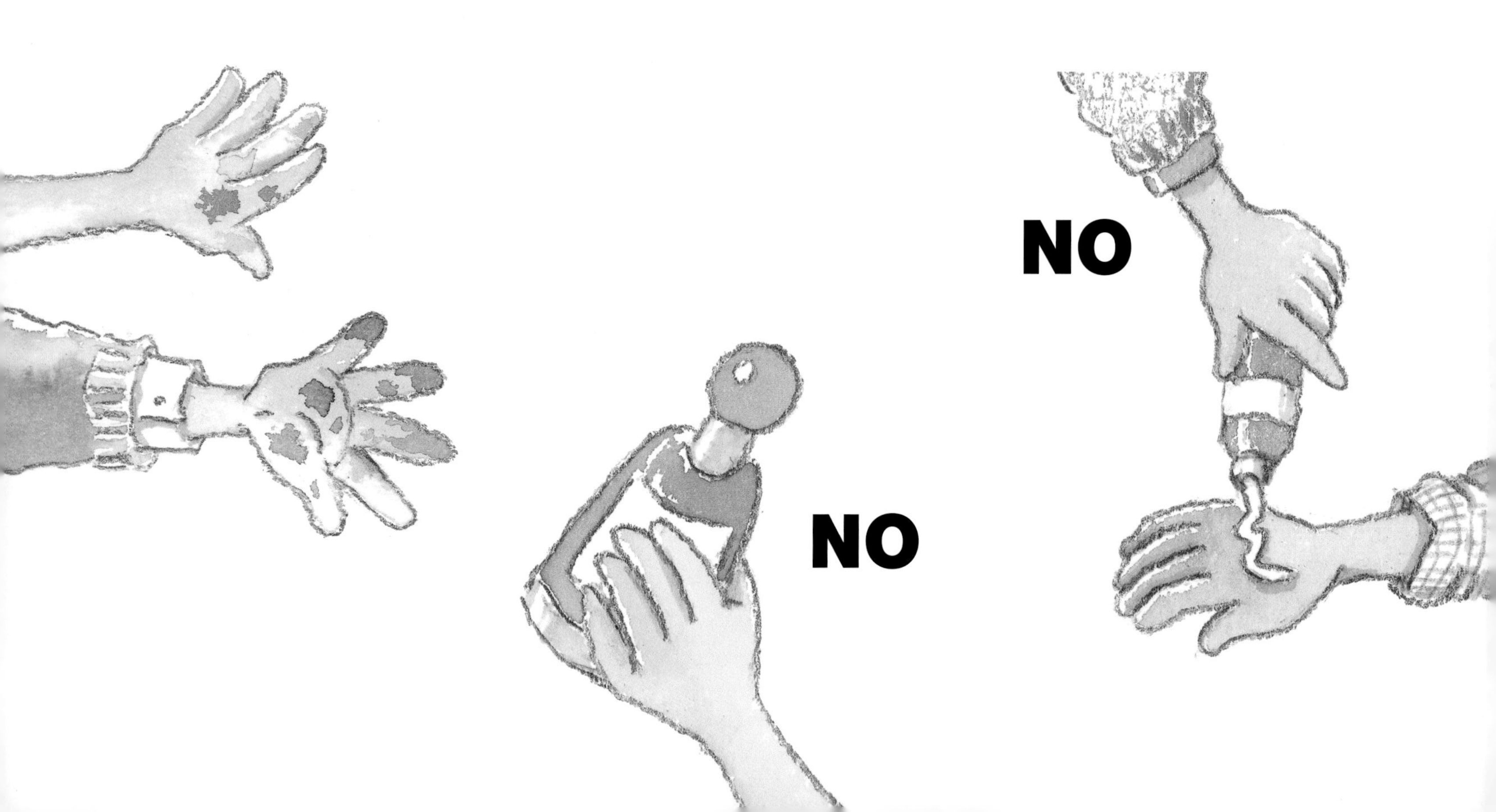

It's not advisable to touch your eyes or mouth after playing with frogs without having washed your hands.

NO

The glandular secretions through the skin of all amphibians are sometimes toxic, especially when they touch your eyes, mouth, or nose.

Dinner time!

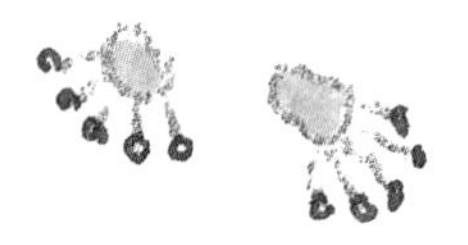

The two frogs love eating insects and small worms. The crickets that Mom brings from the pet shop are their favorite food. As Esmeralda and Prince are still young frogs, they can eat several small crickets per day. When they are fully grown, in about a year, we'll have to give them less food, about four or five large crickets per frog, once every other day. If we gave them all they could eat, they would get very fat! The children are fascinated by watching the two little frogs eat. They are so hungry that as soon as the cricket enters the terrarium, they launch their sticky tongues and . . . gulp! They've already swallowed it!

A nutritious meal

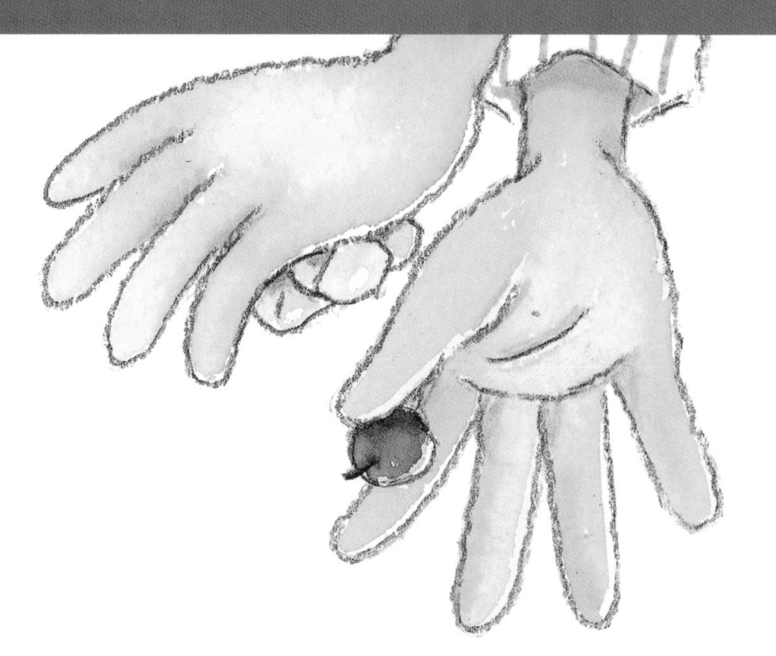

The crickets were a bit "skinny" when they arrived from the pet shop. The day before feeding them to the little frogs, the children gave them some fruit and vegetables. They also gave them some wet dog biscuits, so that the crickets would contain more proteins and water. Esmeralda and Prince thus eat very nutritious prey to make them grow into healthy, strong little frogs.

A couple of times per week, the crickets should be dusted with a special product just before putting them in the terrarium. It's like a white powder, which contains vitamin D and calcium. It's important for your pets to have strong bones.

One foot in front of the other

The White's tree frogs have a very funny way of walking. Throughout the day, they usually stay stuck to the glass or on a high branch, resting from the heat of the lamp. At night, they begin to move about and search for food. When they walk along the branches and plants, they place one foot in front of the other (or "hand over hand"), advancing gradually.

They also jump sometimes, though this is unusual. Andrea and Albert are captivated by how the two frogs inspect their terrarium at nightfall.

A very clean terrarium

Esmeralda and Prince are quite clean animals, but their terrarium must be kept clean at all times. Their bath water should be changed every day or when dirty. Mineral water or tap water without chlorine should be used. Water straight from the tap is not good, because the chlorine in it can harm the frogs. Distilled water is also not good for the frogs.

The terrarium glass should be cleaned with water, rubbing with a damp cloth.

Every day, Andrea and Albert remove the dry leaves and dead crickets from the floor of the terrarium.

Color changes

Each frog is a specific color: Esmeralda is an intense green color; Prince is brown. But they don't always have the same tone. They sometimes assume the color of the leaves and branches of their terrarium. They also get scared and depending on the temperature of their surroundings, slight color changes can occur in their bodies.

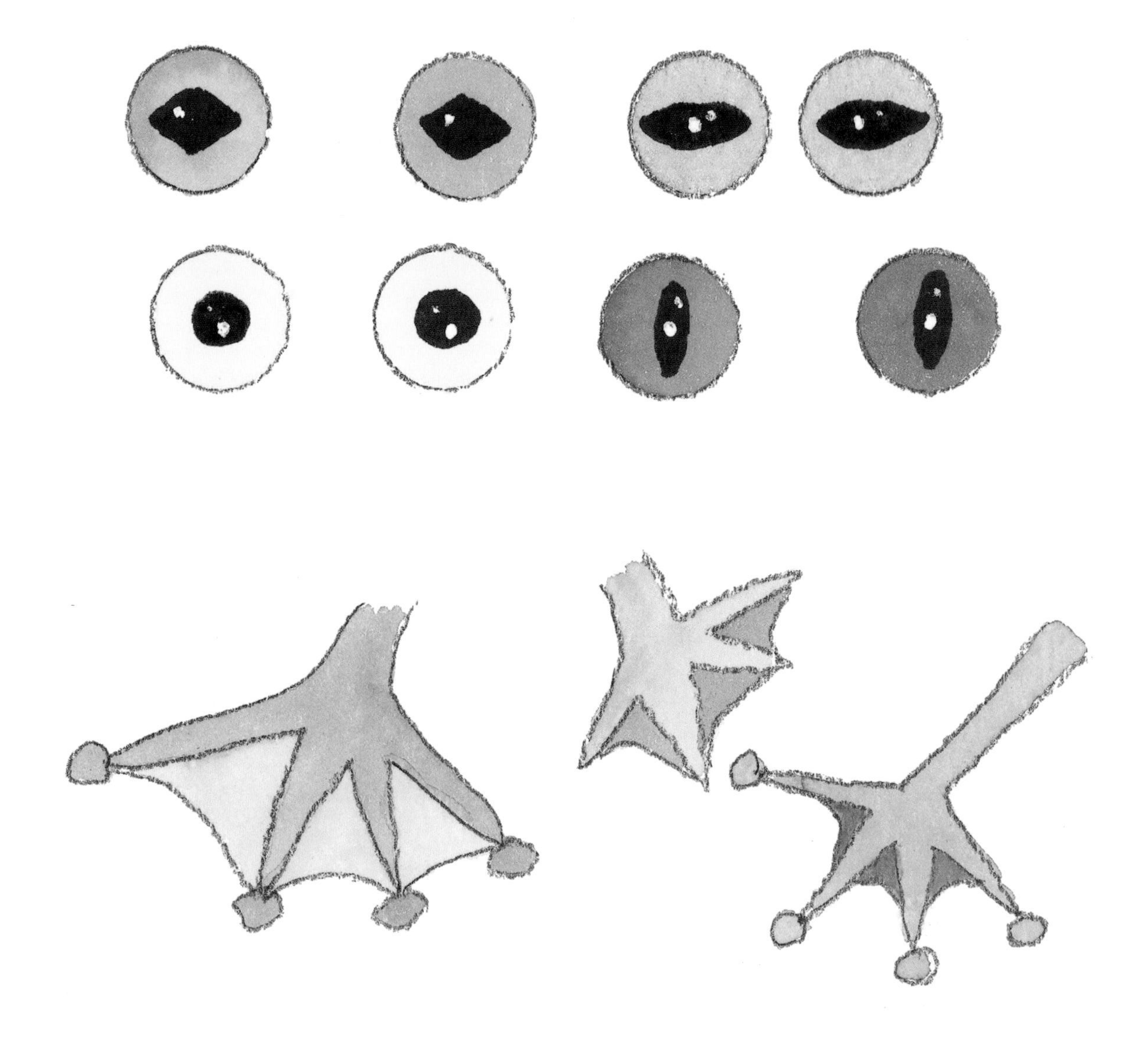

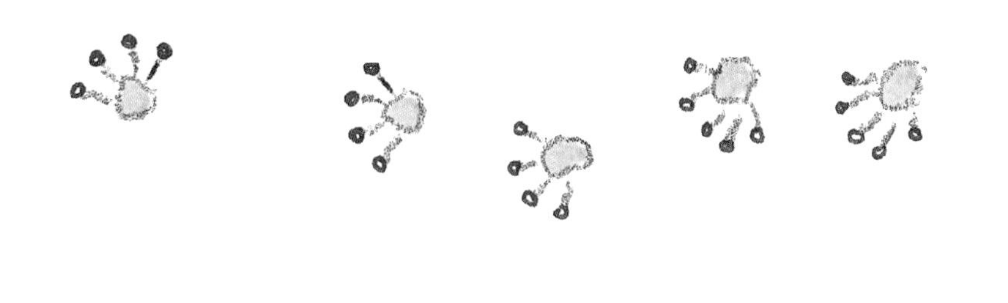

Both their bellies are always a whitish color, without changing. Their eyes are golden, with horizontal black pupils. What pretty eyes! The treefrogs always appear alert!

How frogs sing!

Like many other frogs from all over the world, Esmeralda and Prince "sing" at certain times of the year: namely, spring and summer. It appears that Prince is a male frog: At night, he sings from high up in a branch where he is resting. It's not an unpleasant sound; it's a low-pitched "croak-croak-croak." Esmeralda is quieter, though the children have heard her sometimes. When the frogs are scared they emit a sharp unpleasant cry. Perhaps Esmeralda is a female, though it's not easy to tell.

Nature's best lesson

Albert and Andrea are going to learn nature's best lesson. By looking after their frogs, they will learn that a pet is not a toy. They will learn that animals should be treated well, so that they feel comfortable living with us and don't get scared. As the years go by, they will become very fond of them and will know better than anyone how frogs behave, how they live, and what they need. Sometimes, the smallest creatures teach us the most important lesson: Respecting life.

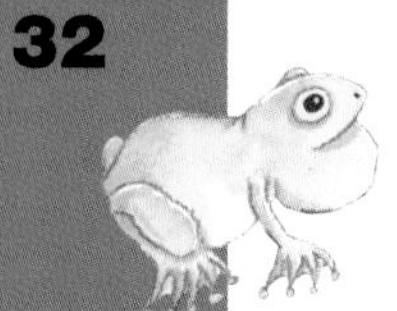

The Frog Game

MATERIALS: Cardboard, scissors, crayons, string

PLAYERS: At least two

1. Players draw and paint their own frogs, similar to the one in the illustration.
2. Each player cuts out the drawing, makes a hole (as shown), and passes a 20-inch (50 cm) string through it.
3. Each player must attempt to step on the frogs of the other players until he or she tears them away from their strings. The winner is the one whose frog survives the longest.

Advice from the veterinarian

Can we have a frog as a pet?
Amphibians in general (frogs, toads, salamanders, and newts) are delicate animals, most of which need a damp environment, because if their skin dries, they will die. However, having them as pets has become popular and quite a lot of amphibians can now be found in pet shops. The Australian green tree frog, also called White's tree frog, has many favorable characteristics making it an ideal frog for beginners, as it is relatively simple to look after and is quite resilient.

How to choose your little frog
The day you go to the pet shop to buy your White's tree frog, you should consider some advice. Above all, you should be aware that your new little friend is going to keep you company for several years, if all goes well. It can live for ten years, easily reaching fifteen.

Individuals with a healthy appearance should be selected, with uniform skin with no scuff marks or abnormal lumps. It is also important that they demonstrate normal behavior, tranquil but alert (be wary if, for example, it is lying down asleep in the middle of the terrarium). It's difficult to distinguish between male and female frogs, at least for non-experts and it's even more complicated when dealing with young specimens.

A comfortable and cozy terrarium
It's very important to prepare an adequate terrarium for your White's tree frog. To house two adult frogs, the capacity of the enclosure should be no less than 10 gallons (40 liters) of water; in any case, the bigger the terrarium, the better. A vertically built terrarium is preferable (higher than it is wide), as the little frog loves to climb up the plants and trunks inside it. The decoration can either be artificial or living plants ("pothos" are a good choice). Several branches and trunks should be positioned horizontally so that the frog can climb and have a place to lie down in the heat. If the decoration comes from outdoors, it must be well cleaned. If artificial elements are used, you must be certain that they are not painted or varnished, as chipped paint or varnish can be fatal for your pets. It is advisable to cover three or four walls of the terrarium (the back and sides), using the decorated paper on sale in pet shops. A very important aspect to be considered is the terrarium lid, made from mesh to facilitate the passage of air. It must be closable in a safe way, otherwise the little frog will be able to escape.

More things about your little frog's house
It's important to maintain the terrarium temperature controlled within certain limits, especially if you live in a cold zone or with relatively harsh winters. With a lamp (not too bright) placed in the upper part of the terrarium, outside the mesh cover, a daytime temperature of between 80.6° and 86°F (27 and 30°C) should be maintained. To obtain this, try different light bulb strengths and altering the distance between the lamp and the terrarium. At night, the temperature may drop to 64° to 68°F (18–20°C) with no problems; generally, with the lamp switched off, the room temperature is sufficient. A cycle of 12 hours of light to 12 hours of darkness is appropriate. Regarding the terrarium substratum, there are several options, though it's always best to avoid materials that the frog could swallow accidentally, like gravel or sawdust. Soil, free from fertilizers and pesticides can be used and plants can even be planted directly in it. It's also advisable to add moss. The frogs need a container of fresh water, so they can cool down whenever they want. You should use mineral water or at least water without chlorine (this can be obtained by leaving tap water in an uncovered container for two days). This "bath" water should not cover the entire frog, but just the legs and it should be able to get out of the container

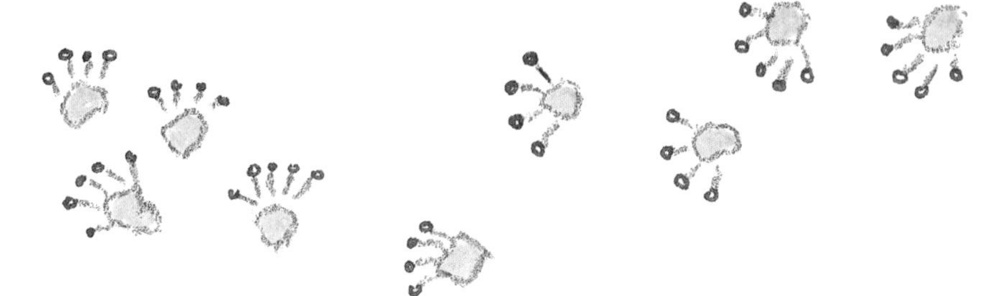

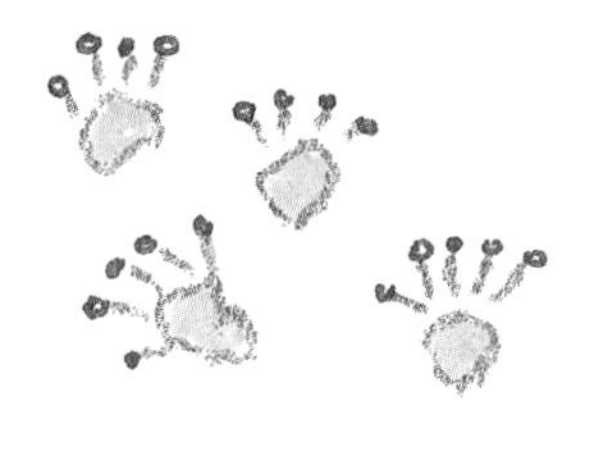

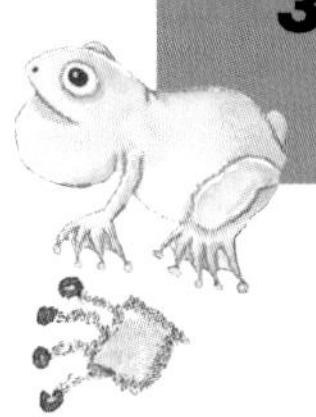

easily. The White's tree frog is not a very good swimmer and could drown. Finally, you should consider the humidity of the terrarium. As opposed to other amphibians, they don't need too much humidity, though they always need a little, especially during the hot months. The terrarium should be sprinkled regularly with water and you should check that evaporated water does not condense on the glass, indicating that the enclosure is too humid.

Food

Like the rest of the amphibians, the White's tree frog is a voracious insectivore. If you don't regulate what you give it to eat, it can get fat very quickly. In the wild, these frogs eat all kinds of non-poisonous insects, like moths, flies, cockroaches, crickets, and also caterpillars and worms. The largest examples may rarely even eat other small frogs. You can feed your pet crickets, sold in pet shops, as you can be sure that their food is not contaminated with insecticides. An occasional earthworm or silk worms are appetizing dishes with which to vary their diet. Remember that they only eat live animals. You should follow this important rule when feeding your frog: You should never give it prey longer than its mouth, to avoid problems when swallowing. The crickets available in pet shops tend to be "skinny" and not very nutritious. It's necessary to "fatten them up" with nutritious food before giving them to your pet. You can feed them on dog food, supplemented with fruit and vegetables, such as orange, apple, lettuce, potato, and carrot. Special products can also be found for fattening up crickets—ask in your pet shop. You should dust the crickets with a supplement of calcium and vitamins before placing them in the terrarium about once a week. This will make the frogs grow healthy and with strong bones. Young frogs can eat as many small crickets per day as they like; you can feed adult frogs four or five crickets once every other day.

Handling the frog

The White's tree frog, like the rest of the amphibians, has delicate skin which must be kept humid in order to survive. Though touching your pet cannot harm you, it's best not to leave it in contact with your skin for a very long time and you should never put it near your face. Glandular secretions CAN irritate eyes and mucous membranes, especially if the frog is stressed. These frogs are very docile and don't object to being picked up; lift them very carefully, of course. You should always wash your hands before touching them. You should remove any traces of soap from your hands, rinsing them with lots of water and drying them thoroughly with a towel, as traces of soap can be absorbed by the frog's skin and be fatal. It can also harm them if you wear perfume, creams, or any other type of product on your hands. That's why it's important to insist on washing before you pick them up. It's equally important to wash your hands when you've finished with them and not touch your eyes or mouth until you have done so.

Any aerosol, like insecticides and soap of any type can quickly be fatal for your little frogs. When you clean the terrarium walls, use water alone. If you use any type of cleaning product, you must rinse several times with water, so that no traces remain.

How big are they? Can I keep several frogs together?

The White's tree frogs have different sizes depending on their sex. The females are generally larger and can exceed 4 inches (10 cm) long (without counting their back legs). The males, on the other hand, are usually smaller: About 2.75 inches (7 cm) at adult age. You can keep several frogs of both sexes in the same terrarium, though the more frogs you have, the bigger the terrarium should be. The most important thing is to never mix small young frogs with large ones, as the young may end up being eaten by the older ones. They should always be of a similar size to live together.

LET'S TAKE CARE OF OUR NEW FROG

First edition for the United States and Canada published in 2008 by Barron's Educational Series, Inc.

Original title of the book in Catalan: *Una rana en casa*
© Copyright GEMSER PUBLICATIONS S.L., 2007
c/Castell, 38 Teià (08329) Barcelona, Spain (World Rights)
Tel: 93 540 13 53
E-mail: info@mercedesros.com
Author: Alejandro Algarra
Illustrator: Rosa María Curto

All rights reserved.
No part of this book may be reproduced in any form, by photostat, microfilm, xerography, or any other means, or incorporated into any information retrieval system, electronic or mechanical without the written permission of the copyright owner.

All inquiries should be addressed to:
Barron's Educational Series, Inc.
250 Wireless Boulevard
Hauppauge, New York 11788
www.barronseduc.com

ISBN-13: 978-0-7641-3879-9
ISBN-10: 0-7641-3879-0

Library of Congress Control No.: 2007936437

Printed in China
9 8 7 6 5 4 3 2 1